The To
and the Hare

Retold by Margo Lundell
Illustrated by John Nez

A GOLDEN BOOK • NEW YORK

Western Publishing Company, Inc., Racine, Wisconsin 53404

Once there was a hare who lived in a wood. The hare thought of himself as a very clever fellow.

Often the hare visited his friend the tortoise. He liked to tell his friend how clever he was.

One day the hare came to the tortoise's house to show off five plump turnips he had taken from the farmer's garden. "How smart of me," said the hare, "to find such turnips."

The next day the hare spent half the afternoon looking at himself in the stream.

"What fine ears I have," said the hare. "How handsome I am."

On the following day the hare told the tortoise that he had run away from the farmer that very morning. "I am surely the fastest runner there is," he bragged.

At last the tortoise had heard enough boasting.
"I know you can run very fast," she said. "But
I could beat you in a race."

The hare laughed, and danced about on his fine strong legs. "You? The slowpoke?" he said. "You think you can beat me? Nonsense."

"Believe what you will," said the tortoise. "But
tomorrow we shall race each other—all the way
to the top of the far hill."

The next day everyone gathered to watch the race. No one thought the tortoise could win. But the owl, who was the judge, simply said, "We shall see."

"Go!" said the owl, and the race was on.

The tortoise plodded forward on her short, stubby legs.

The hare leapt out in front. Before anyone could say "Jackrabbit," he was out of sight.

The hare ran past flowering meadows and grassy fields.

He sped by the apple orchard and on down the road.

Just before he reached the finish line, the hare stopped. He stretched out in the warm sun behind a tall hedge to wait for the tortoise.

The tortoise kept up her slow, steady pace. She passed the flowering meadows and grassy fields.

She reached the apple orchard and kept going.

At last the tortoise neared
the finish line.

But she wondered, "Where is
the hare?" He was fast asleep
behind the hedge!

"Hurray!" shouted the animals as the tortoise finished the race.

The hare awoke with a start. He couldn't believe his eyes. The tortoise was taking a bow.

"I was here hours ago," said the hare. "I fell asleep behind the hedge."

"But I crossed the finish line ahead of you,"
said the tortoise.

"True, true," said the judge. "The tortoise is
the winner."

The owl had something else to add. "Slow and
steady often wins the race," he said.
And the tortoise and the hare agreed.